No Place for a Goat

by Helen Roney Sattler • illustrated by Bari Weissman

ELSEVIER/NELSON BOOKS
New York

Dedicated to Bob
who also knew and loved Sam

Library of Congress Catalog Card Number 80-26558   ISBN 0-525-66723-7
Published in the United States by Elsevier-Dutton Publishing Co., Inc.,
2 Park Avenue, New York, N.Y. 10016.
Printed in the U.S.A.   First edition

10 9 8 7 6 5 4 3 2 1

Sam walked around and around the house. He was looking for a way to get in. He was sure there was a way. And if there was, he was going to find it.

Even though he was Joey's pet goat, Sam wasn't allowed inside the house. He was very curious about it. Now it is all right to be curious about some things. And it is all right to be curious sometimes. But Sam was curious about everything all the time.

Once, when he found the back door open, he walked right up and looked into the house through the screen door. He saw the pretty curtains at the windows, and the bright red tablecloth. He saw the pretty yellow flowers in pots. He saw all kinds of nice things.

Good smells came from inside the house, too. Sam could smell rolls baking in the oven and a fine dinner cooking.

He could hear the big clock ticking and water running in the sink. And he could hear music and a ringing telephone.

If only he could get in!

But Sam didn't know how to get into the house. When he tried
to get in with Joey, Joey's mother stopped him.

"Joey, don't let that goat in," she said.

"Can't he come in for just a little while?" Joey asked.

"No, he can't come in," his mother answered. "He is a goat
and our house is no place for a goat."

I will have to find another way, thought Sam.

And one day, Sam was sure he had found it. Someone had piled some wood against the garage. Sam jumped up on the wood. Then he jumped onto the garage roof. He was so excited! He couldn't help it—he did a little dance right there. Then he ran to the chimney. He stood on his hind legs to look down it. Then—

"Sam! Get off that roof! You silly goat!" cried Joey's mother. Sam got down. But he did not give up. There *must* be a way to get in, he thought. And if there is, I will find it.

Around and around the house he went. He looked and looked.
Then he found something. He found a hole in the screen door.
He knew he had only to wait for a time when no one was home.

Sam knew how to wait. He waited and waited. And at last Joey
left for school. Then his mother got into the car and drove away.
No one was home.

Sam ran to the screen door. The hole was still there. The wooden door was open.

Then he heard something. It was tires on the drive. Joey's mother had come back. Sam ran behind the garage, but he was too late. Joey's mother saw him.

"Sam, I forgot to tie you up," she said. "I don't know what you might get into, if I left you untied." She tied Sam to a tree with a rope. Then she got into the car and drove away again.

Sam was so mad! He hated to be tied up. Most of all, he was mad because he couldn't get into the house. But soon he saw that he was tied with a rope — and goats can eat ropes. Sam chewed the rope in two. It tasted very good. But he wanted to taste the things in the house, so he left the rope for another time.

He ran to the house. The hole in the screen was still there. Sam looked around. He listened. He heard nothing but the big clock. TICKTOCK, TICKTOCK, TICKTOCK.

Sam put his head through the hole. That was easy. He put a leg in. That wasn't so easy. He put another leg in. He heard a loud RIP. Then he was in the house.

Sam was so excited! He couldn't help it—he did a little dance.
His feet made such lovely sounds on the floor. CLICK, CLICK,
CLIPPITY CLOP.

He jumped upon the table and did another dance. Dishes flew everywhere. They made such nice noises as they fell to the floor. CLICK, CLICK, CLIPPITY CLOP, CRASH, BANG, KER-SPLAT! Oh, it was such fun!

Sam tasted the curtains. He tasted the rug. He tasted a blanket.
He didn't like them very much, but the yellow flowers were very
good.

Sam jumped upon the sofa. Oh, what fun! Up, up, up he went.
Up and down, down and up. But he jumped one time too many

and a little too hard. He landed ker-plop on his face on the floor.
He didn't like that!

Sam got up and started down the hall just as Joey's mother came in the front door.

"Sam! You get out of this house!" she cried.

Sam ran down the hall. He bumped into the big clock. It fell on top of him. It was heavy and it hurt. BONG, BONG, BONG, it went. How frightened Sam was!

He crawled out from under the clock and backed into the telephone stand. A tall vase of flowers fell over and water poured down on his head. It ran into his eyes. Sam couldn't see where he

was going. He tripped over the vacuum cleaner. It growled at him and grabbed his ear. Sam thought it would swallow his whole head! How terrible it was!

Sam wanted to be outside. He wasn't curious about the inside of the house any more. Just as Joey's mother seized a broom, Sam saw an open door and dashed through it. But it was the wrong door. He was trapped in a closet. The horrible broom landed on his back.

"Get out, get out," Joey's mother kept yelling, as she chased him with the broom.

I'm going, I'm going, as soon as I can find the right door, thought Sam. But as he ran around looking for it, his feet slipped on the wet floor and he crashed into a wall. Then, as he dashed

into the kitchen, he bumped into the hot oven. It burned his nose.
He stepped back on a spoon. His feet flew out from under him
and he landed on his bottom, ker-plop, on a fork! Oh, that hurt!

"It serves you right," Joey's mother said. "A house is no place for a goat."

You know, thought Sam, as he limped through the door at last, she is *right*!